Pop Pop

Zanzibar

Dad

Maya

My Big Barefoot Book of

WONDERFUL WORDS

Felix

Sam

Crunchy

Mom

For my family:
Nick, Sasha, Darrin
and Pammy Jane
— K. M. J. D.

For Anna Andrisani,
Antonio Amato, Mara,
Palma, Carmen and Enzo,
such a wonderful family!
— S. F.

Barefoot Books
2067 Massachusetts Ave
Cambridge, MA 02140

Text copyright © 2014 by Barefoot Books
Illustrations copyright © 2014 by Sophie Fatus
The moral rights of Barefoot Books
and Sophie Fatus have been asserted

First published in the United States of America
by Barefoot Books, Inc in 2014
All rights reserved

Graphic design by Katie Jennings Campbell,
Asheville, North Carolina, USA
Reproduction by B & P International, Hong Kong
Printed in China on 100% acid-free paper
This book was typeset in Slappy
The illustrations were prepared in
mixed media: acrylic and colored pencils

Hardback ISBN 978-1-78285-092-2
First Book paperback ISBN 978-1-78285-168-4

Library of Congress Cataloging-
in-Publication Data
is available under LCCN 2013030851

1 3 5 7 9 8 6 4 2

My Big Barefoot Book of
WONDERFUL WORDS

Sophie Fatus

Barefoot Books
step inside a story

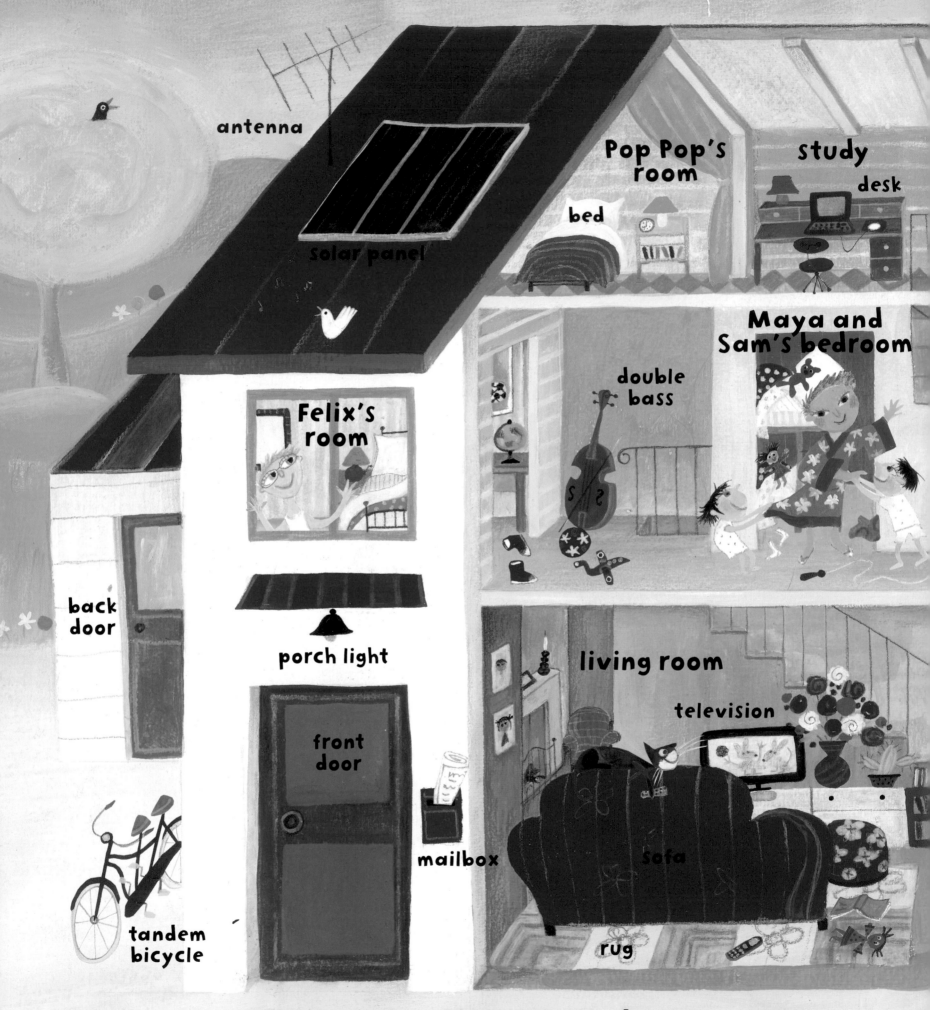

It's morning time at our house.
The birds are chirping.

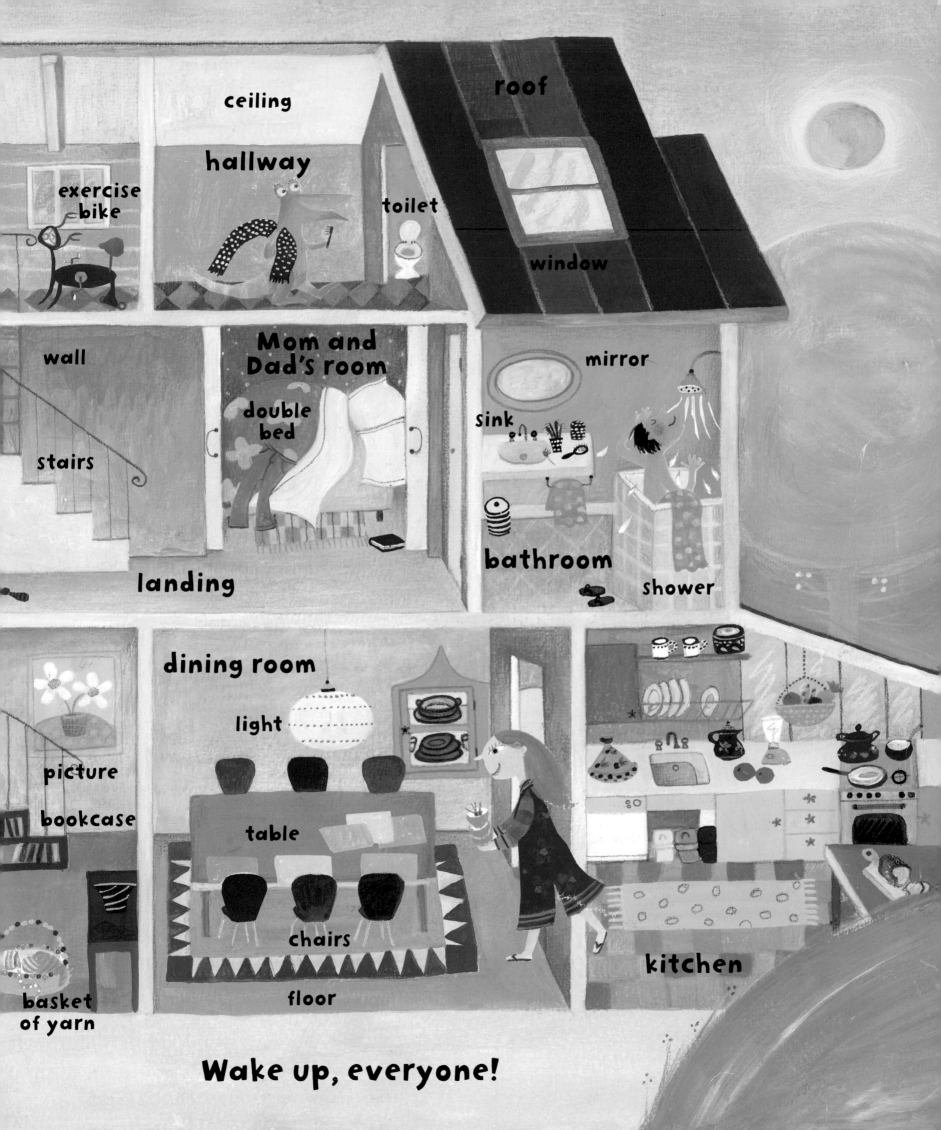

roof

ceiling

hallway

exercise bike

toilet

window

wall

Mom and Dad's room

mirror

double bed

sink

stairs

bathroom

shower

landing

dining room

light

picture

bookcase

table

chairs

kitchen

basket of yarn

floor

Wake up, everyone!

Let's get dressed!

baseball cap

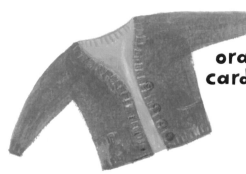
orange cardigan

sarong

mitten missing its mate

white undershirt

red t-shirt

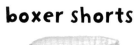
cowboy hat

boxer shorts

pants

yellow raincoat

sneakers

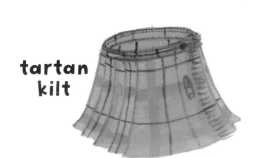
pink party dress

cat

dashiki

tartan kilt

beret

What would you like to wear today?

purple kimono

straw hat

striped tights

gloves

fuzzy earmuffs

gray tracksuit

socks

shorts

shirt

skirt

blue overalls

sandals

green tunic

sari

salwar kameez

brown boots

black shoes

Everyone is making breakfast.
The cocoa smells delicious.

Don't let Crunchy eat the pancakes!

stockpot

hot cocoa

pot

bacon

frying pan

oven

whisk

rocket ship pancakes

mixing bowl

measuring spoons

spoon

fork

sugar bowl

cereal

table

orange juice

bread

butter

toaster

burnt toast

tiles

After breakfast, Mom and Dad go to the shed.

canned tomatoes

wall

pins

mannequin

canning jars

ax

handsaw

fabric bolt

wrench

toolbox

hammer

apron

rag

nails

thread

scissors

paint

palette

workbench

measuring tape

paintbrushes

Dad's old yearbooks

paint cans

paint roller

Pop Pop is reading his newspaper in the backyard.

garden

zucchini

tomato plants

chicken coop

Mavis, Beatrice, Matilda and Lara

beehive

pea plants

shoots

seeds

path

shovel

lettuce

wheelbarrow

hose

hoe

stake

garden fork

wire

arm floaties

baby pool

lawn mower

rake

rain barrel

woodpile

recycling bin

compost bin

trash can

trellis

"Pop Pop, will you take us to the library, please?" asks Sam.

ladybug

butterfly

tree

clothesline

clothespins

tire swing

lawn

newspaper

lawn chair

bush

"And then can we go to the park?" asks Maya.

carrot

potato

turnip

beet

brussels sprouts

spinach

green beans

tomatoes

green peas

corn

yellow squash

broccoli

cauliflower

lettuce

"Sure!" says Pop Pop. "Let's go to town.
But first, let's pick some vegetables."

pumpkin

okra

celery

asparagus

onion

leek

cucumber

yucca

garlic

avocados

artichoke

peppers

zucchini

cabbage

kale

sweet potato

It's a sunny day. The streets are busy.

boutique

hotel

café

art gallery

police station

florist

doctor's office

animal shelter

vegetable stand

bakery

sushi bar

delicatessen

bistro

post office

Look at all of these people!

artist

musician

construction worker

architect

writer

editor

farmer

teacher

photographer

bookseller

doctor

carpenter

soccer player

chef

police officer

astronaut

Sam wants to be a chef.

acrobat

ballet dancer

firefighter

vet

mechanic

judge

reporter

bus driver

arborist

actor

potter

hair stylist

fashion designer

What do you want to be when you grow up?

Look! It's a construction site.

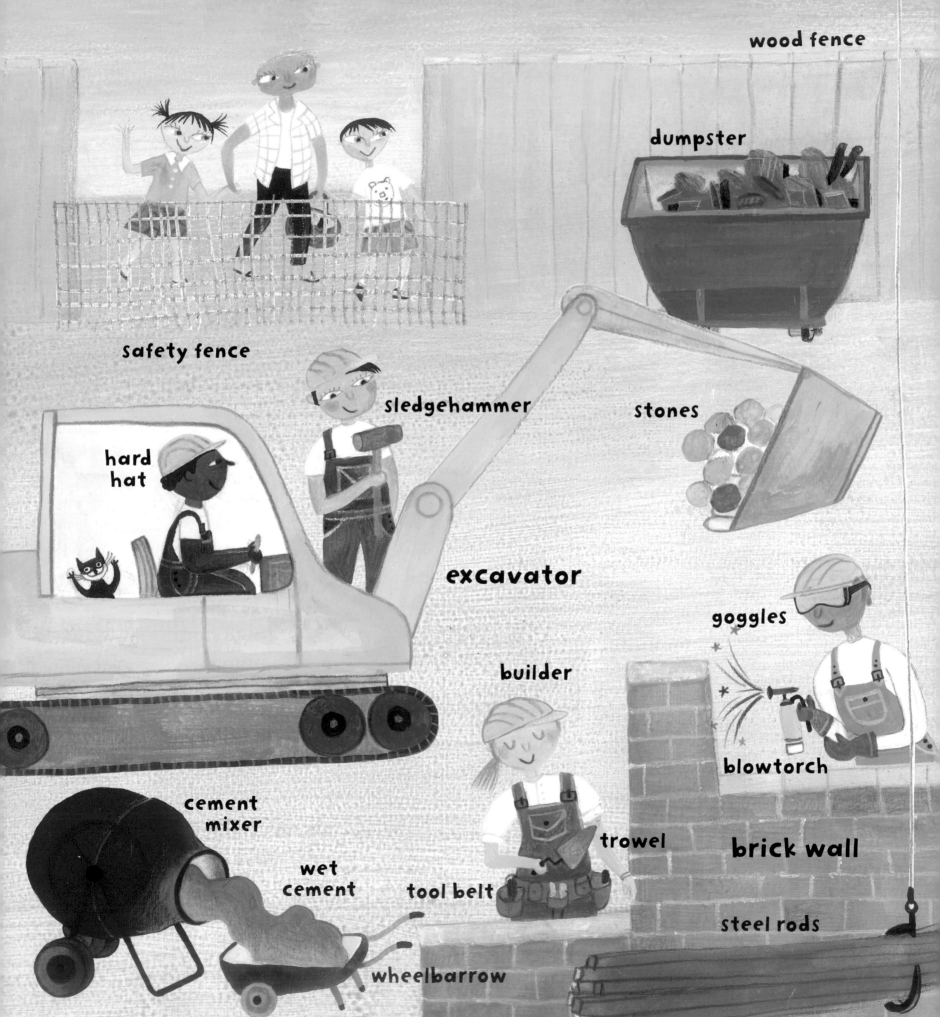

wood fence

dumpster

safety fence

sledgehammer

stones

hard hat

excavator

goggles

builder

blowtorch

cement mixer

trowel

brick wall

wet cement

tool belt

steel rods

wheelbarrow

crane

forklift

bulldozer

sandbags

orange cones

jackhammer

foreman

architect

blueprints

buckets

square

scaffolding

Pop Pop says they're
building a new house here.

What kind of home would you like to live in?

castle

houseboat

mansion

igloo

stilt house

tree house

Scottish croft

bell tent

town house

trailer

tepee

apartment building

A-frame

palace

hut

thatched cottage

terraced house

farmhouse

eco house

cave

geodesic dome

log cabin

poster

coatrack

media

bulletin board

bookshelves

books

leaflets

stuffed kangaroo

screen

hearing aid loop sign

keyboard

dictionary

notebook

computer

mouse

mouse pad

globe

computer desk

headphones

trash can

At the library, Mr. Thomas helps us choose some books to read.

bookcase

lost-and-found box

magazines

librarian

rubber stamp

circulation desk

book return

origami bird

paper boat

Braille book

scissors

crayons

pipe cleaners

stickers

paper plates

craft tables

Sam likes stories with lots of magic in them.

Which story characters would you like to meet?

angel

warrior

alien

fairy

prince

elf

giant

griffin

goblin

dragon

knight

ghost

princess

troll

vampire

queen

king

spy

witch

wizard

robber

mermaid

unicorn

At the market, Pop Pop
buys a jar of golden honey.
"This looks like a good one," he says.

meat

pork

mushrooms

books

herbs

spices

Gouda

Roquefort

Cheddar

goat cheese

cheeses

Brie

mozzarella

eggs

twine

meat cleaver

lamb

steak

beef

butcher's block

wax paper

candy

fruit

scale

oranges

apples

grapes

kiwi

bananas

pineapples

baguettes

flowers

wreath

tulips

sunflowers

daisies

roses

poultry

lavender

hens

duck

carnations

It's full of children playing. Let's join in!

somersault

sandwich

ants

carrots

lemonade

picnic basket

thermos

hummus

animal crackers

picnic blanket

skateboard

seesaw

jump rope

grass

rope swing

hopscotch

swing

Everyone in the park looks happy and relaxed.

sad

bored

impatient

embarrassed

puzzled

calm

thoughtful

angry

offended

jealous

curious

disgusted

annoyed

hungry

hopeful

sleepy

nervous

patient

happy

scared

wary

excited

loving

sick

lonely

How do you think these children feel?

It's time to go home now.

walk signal

sidewalk   manhole

road

STOP

crossing guard   crosswalk   lamppost

pedicab

flag

billboard

church   bus stop

Look—our bus is coming. Hurry!

There are so many ways to get around.

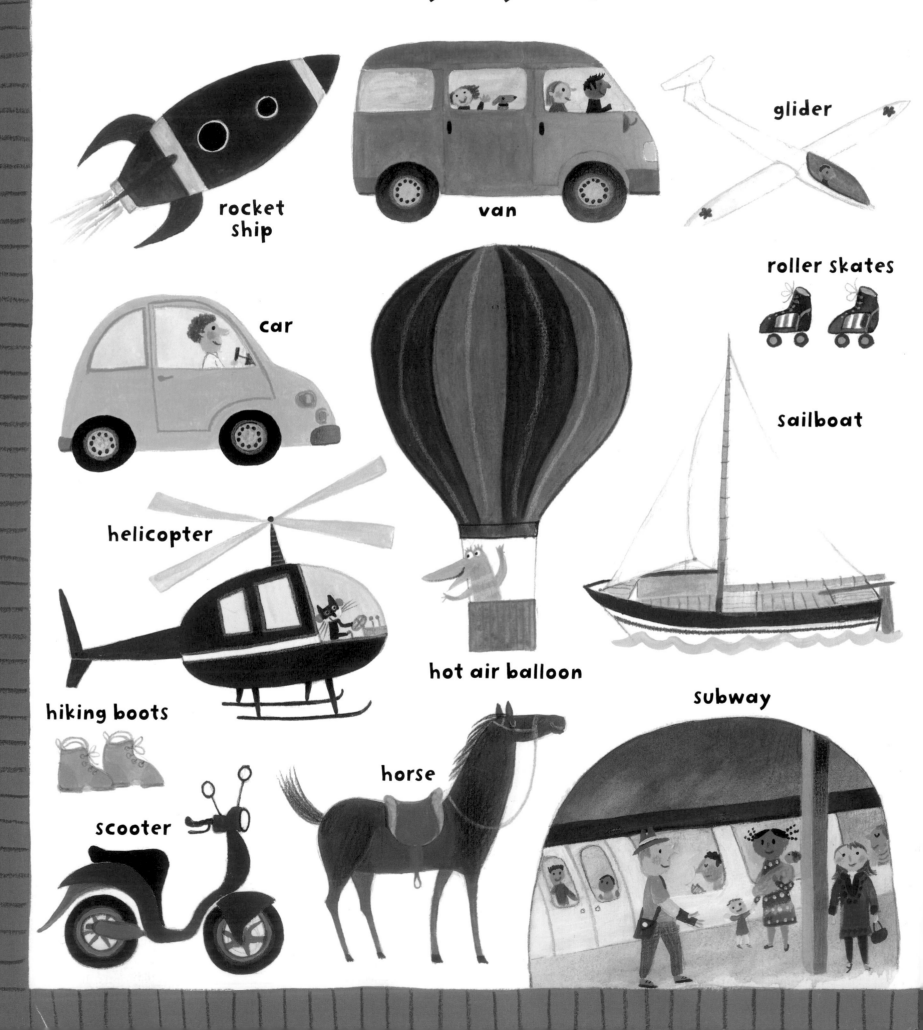

rocket ship

van

glider

roller skates

car

sailboat

helicopter

hot air balloon

subway

hiking boots

horse

scooter

How do you like to travel?

barge

train

rowboat

vintage
sports car

airplane

motorcycle

truck

skateboards

bicycle

fire engine

police car

bus

llamas

hills

field

bridge

tractor

trailer

silo

river

scarecrow

hay bale

farmer

chickens

corn

combine
harvester

cyclist

On the way home, we drive
through the country.

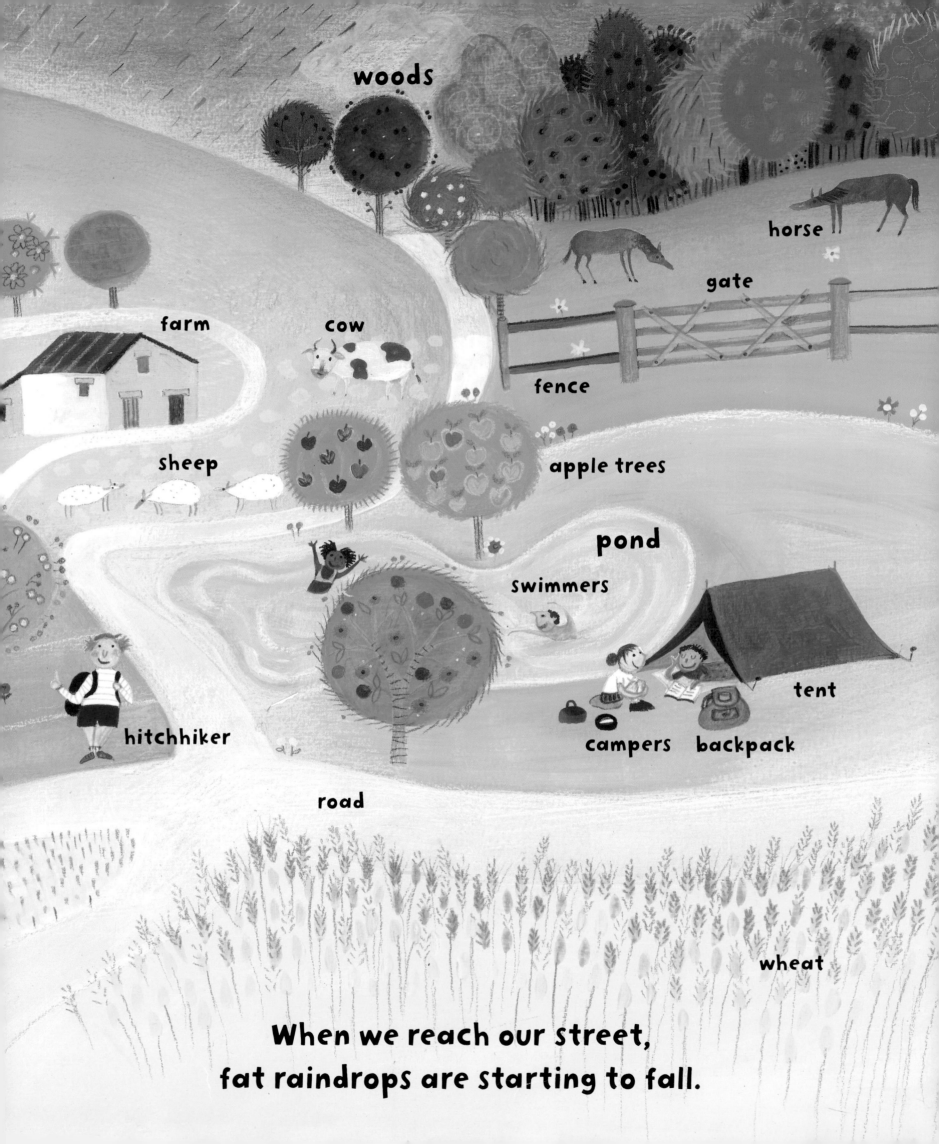

woods

horse

gate

farm

cow

fence

sheep

apple trees

pond

swimmers

tent

hitchhiker

campers   backpack

road

wheat

When we reach our street,
fat raindrops are starting to fall.

It looks like there's going to be a storm!

clouds

fog

hail

ice

barometer

drizzle

sleet

tornado

umbrella

wind sock

What is your favorite kind of weather?

frost

hurricane

rain

sun

snow

weather vane

rainbow

blizzard

wind

thunderstorm

lightning

A rainy night is perfect for spending time together.

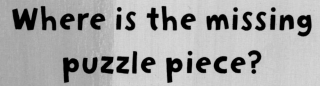

Where is the missing puzzle piece?

painting

candle

mirror

photograph

logs

fireplace

bellows

chess

cushion

lamp
shade

deck of
cards

lightbulb

chair

Maya's book is all about animals.

dog

yak

buffalo

xoona moth

elephant

umbrella bird

wolf

anteater

quail

giraffe

parrot

meerkat

nightingale

snake

vulture

zebra

rhinoceros

chimpanzee

jackal

ibex

kangaroo

flamingo

orangutan

lion

tiger

hippopotamus

Which animal would you like to have as a pet?
Can you put the animals in alphabetical order?

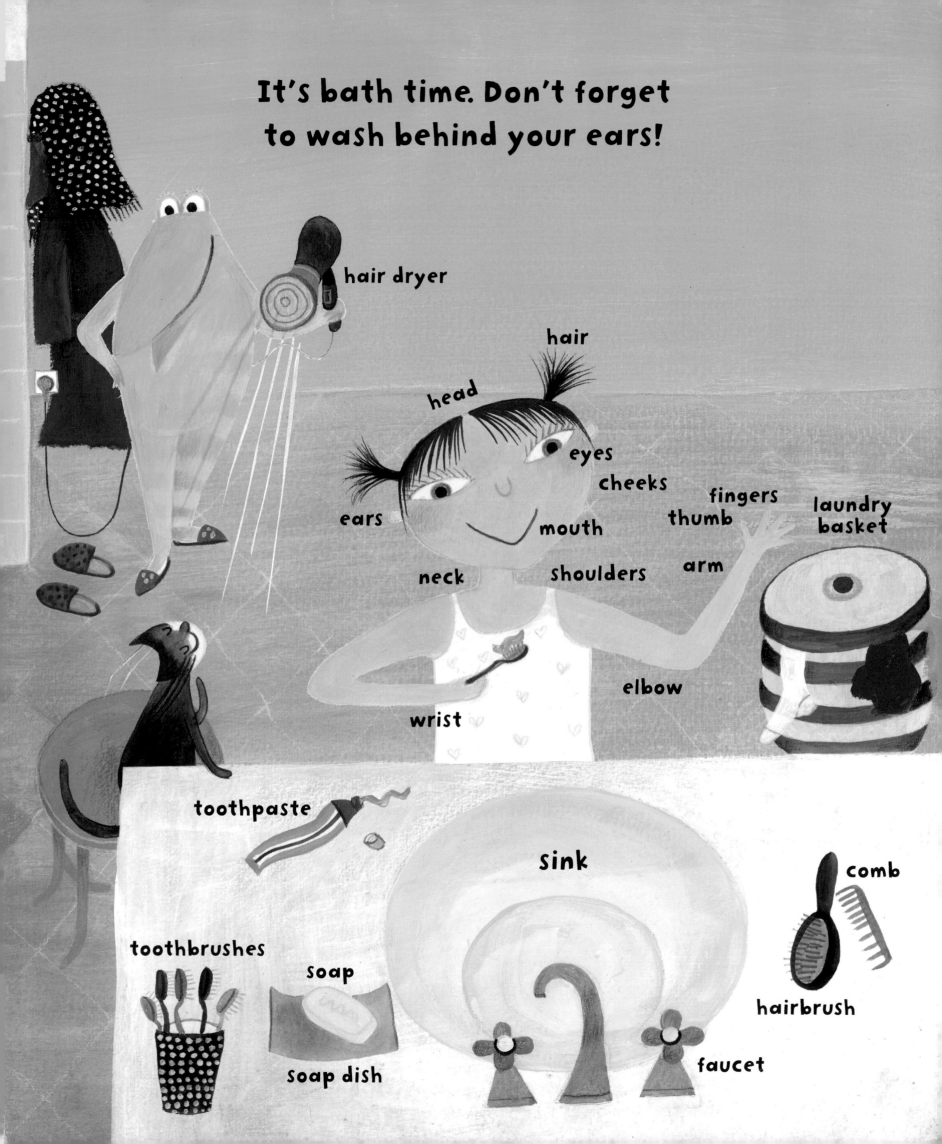

It's bath time. Don't forget
to wash behind your ears!

Barefoot Books
step inside a story

At Barefoot Books, we celebrate art and story that opens the hearts
and minds of children from all walks of life, focusing on themes that
encourage independence of spirit, enthusiasm for learning and respect
for the world's diversity. The welfare of our children is dependent on
the welfare of the planet, so we source paper from sustainably managed
forests and constantly strive to reduce our environmental impact.
Playful, beautiful and created to last a lifetime, our products combine
the best of the present with the best of the past to educate our
children as the caretakers of tomorrow.

www.barefootbooks.com